Girl, Cow

&

Monk

Kate Wyer

Meekling Press 2020

Meekling Press
Chicago, IL
meeklingpress.com

Printed in the USA.

Cover art by Suzanne Gold.

ISBN 978-1-950987-08-5

Library of Congress Control Number: 2020942121

To A.C.

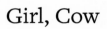
Girl, Cow

1.

Yesterday I combined the stars into a mass larger and brighter than the sun.

Less than half a hemisphere, I told the sun when she was noon, when she was closest to reaching through me.

Remember that, I told her.

*

The cow's great, pale body. Sharp hips. Long ears, sweet ankles. Could I have found a different one? An older one, who knew how to be milked?

What choice was there when my mind said *now*?

I see schools of sardines sleeping in shallows. Their bodies hang, not touching, swaying as if on a mobile. Light builds, fish stir. They begin their elongated roping swim, the sun barely catching their scales. Huge tunas and barracudas know our shadows, our limbs, and the elongated points of our spears.

I look back and take in the pine trees, the wide spaces between them. I see all the way to the houses, to the dark shapes of them. White egrets sleep in high nests, their mating plumage long and wispy from their chests.

The fishermen should be finishing the last of their bitter root coffee and whatever egg or smoked fish they saved for breakfast.

Come, cow, I say to her. *I need a name for you.*
Samira, I tell her. *You'll be Samira.*

She resists, at the water's edge. She blinks her dark eyes and pulls her head back to look longingly toward her pen, her son. My head comes to her shoulder. Samira takes some of my long brown hair into her mouth, chews. I let her.

The night before I left, I said a prayer to the sea to bring me good dreams.

Let me know something of the next months, I said.
Let me know something of the coming year.

I prepared my bed, made a circle of flour around me. The sea did not tell me anything. I did not dream.

2.

A large swell smacks my drum into me. It's doubtful it will dry out enough for me to play it. I had imagined lifting it over my head as we walked along the sandbar that divides the quiet water and the deeps.

In that dream, I was using my mallet and marking time by hitting its skin. Now the thick thump of its leather has no bounce, reverberation. Just wet thuds. I place it on the crown of my head.

We lift our feet from the shore and swim. Samira's good at it, even though she has never done it before. I let her pull me along on the rope until she gets tired. Then I pull her the rest of the way out to the sandbar.

Her body glows under the water as the sun rises. Beds of kelp are in front of us. I see their arms moving and the furred texture of the water. The bladders and wracks like so much webbing. She wades into the sea-weed like it is a chest-high pasture.

The fishermen bring this in for her to eat, so she buries her nose into the dark green and then pulls up a thick mouthful. She tries to chew as water leaves in rivers from her teeth.

Samira relaxes into a cud. *The kelp will keep me for a day*, I think. After that, I will drink her milk.

I have a compass and a sailor's waxed map.

There are saltwater filters in our bodies—the bodies of my ancestors—from decades of sea living. All that is different about our bodies, to the eye, is a slight pouch of our bellies, the slight bloat of water made brackish in our guts.

3.

It is still before noon. I haven't seen anyone clip the periphery. There have been no lunges toward us, no one has seen us walking the horizon. No one has seen us walking away.

I trace my scar, from its origin on my right cheek to its end at my ear and back again. An extended C, a nervous reflex.

The season spent day-by-day in the still rotation of heat fed into water, heat retained.

Samira should be napping in the shade. She moans and blinks her eyes slowly. I see salt collected in her lashes. I want to pet her, but know she will flinch and startle. I stop moving when she stops. She drops her head to sleep and her mouth hits the water. She wakes and then falls again.

I dig my heels into the sea's buoyancy.

I swim to her and then climb on her back, press my arms around her sides with as much pressure as I can manage.

I want to calm her the way I've seen men wrap blankets around her sides, tying them tighter and tighter. I feel the pulse in her throat and her wheezy breaths wet my face. I use the rope and hitch it under her chin to keep her face from hitting the water. She relaxes her jaw muscles and settles the immense weight of her head into my hands. She breathes deeply a few times and sleeps. I take the rope and wrap it around my waist and lean back so I too can rest.

4.

The cow pulls me some, I pull the cow some. We walk this way, if you call it walking. The easy shelf is gone; we wander the sandbar next to the deep pit of cliffs and caverns. To our right, it is now impossible to see the ocean's floor.

Cow-cursing; water-hating; rope-hanging; eye-burning; sun-splicing; south-walking.

I'm quick to forget how solid land feels, and even forget the feeling of air on my legs. How to carry my own weight. What it is like to sit, cross-legged or otherwise, on something that supports me.

The water cools off the shelf and fear is cold too. No one ever said we would be safe out here, they just said we wouldn't drown.

5.

I release the rope from my tight hold and start long strokes from the nape of her neck, all the way down her spine to her hip bones.

Her eyes still half-closed and her body still. I keep at it for a few minutes before I reach along her side. I keep reaching under until I feel her udder. Then I slide off and open my eyes under the water.

The salt stings and clouds my vision, but I keep pushing myself under until I am near her nipples. I pull one out of the water, force it into my mouth. She wakes from her soothed state and starts to walk away from me. She doesn't run.

I've never had hot milk. It is thick and raw, not the cool, thin drink I had after school as a child. It is hard not to choke and spit it all out.

I swallow my mouthful and gasp. Swish some seawater in my mouth and spit.

Samira looks at me and moans. I pull and pull at her body and the water around us becomes cloudy. She moans again.

6.

My favorite time to walk is in the early morning. Samira prefers this too. We walk with the full length of rope between us; me in the front, pulling her forward. She offers the least resistance in the morning. The rest of the day, especially in late afternoon, she won't move. She lets me pull and pull, raise and lower her head with the rope, and stares me down.

I've learned to let her lead and then take us in the other direction.

When I squeeze down on a teat, nothing happens. I try again on another one, and again on a third. All of them have a thick scab over the opening. Peeling it away will cause her intense pain—saltwater in open and cracked skin. I decide to mouth it and soften the crust. She moans loudly and starts to walk away from me.

Her skull is so thick and flat. It feels good on my fingers and my palm when I flatten out my hand and run it up between her ears. She has closed her eyes. I take the large cones of her ears into my hand and stroke their length, twirl around the base, before starting back down to the tip. There is the slightest fringe on the edges. I cup the closed sockets of her eyes and brush salt out of the lashes. Once they are free of their grittiness, I rub down and in a circle, over and over again.

7.

There is no living motion under our feet, not like the silver trains of fish that occasionally stream through our legs in the day.

We enter a thick grove of kelp and stop to eat. This too is for me, to sustain us for the rest of our walk to the most foreign shore I can manage. Samira begins to chew. I try to soften the fibers in my tired jaw.

Would Samira allow me some of her masticated food? Like a baby bird. How do I get it out of her mouth?

I wait until she has taken a large mouthful and is deep in the pleasure of chewing, then grasp one arm of it and tug on it with a quick, sharp motion. Her teeth are too blunt and strong. They come down on the piece and turn it around in her mouth in their side-to-side, slight back and forth motion. I can't take it from the meaty muscle of her tongue.

As I walk through the dense vines, I feel a different texture brush my arm. Skate eggs, hanging in their little black purses, are suspended along one of the plants. The thin arms of the purses are wrapped around the knobby pockets of seaweed. I've never eaten one. I don't think there is much in them, the tiniest of embryos.

It is about half the size of my palm lengthwise, and half widthwise. I can close my hand around it easily.

I gently squeeze the sack between my middle finger and thumb. It feels like there is gel, or some kind of thick liquid. Nothing solid, not even a pearl of life. Just a soup of matter.

My stomach turns at the thought of it. Yet, there is so much walking left. Maybe I should collect as many as I can fit in the drumhead and carry them until I have no better choice.

No. I don't want the opportunity to hold the egg to the sun and look through it to see the start of a winged and tailed fish. I don't want to see even the slightest bend of light through a gill.

I take the purse and gnaw through the leather. My

16

canine tooth punctures it and fluid starts to leak. I bite down harder before I can regret it, and then tear the hole bigger. I can squeeze it out into my mouth. It tastes like an oyster: salty and mineral-rich.

It's not bad. It's not good either, but I can take it over gnawing on kelp.

I collect as many as I can by diving as far as my body will allow me. I feel along the edges of the seaweed trees and reach into the absolute blackness there, plucking them as my hands brush their strange shape. I place them inside the drumhead I have floating upside down.

My teeth have a film on them.

8.

We aren't supposed to be able to drown, but one child did.

A tide came and took him away from the edge of the beach. The child thought the tide was playing with him as it spun him around and pulled him out further into the dark water off the coastal shelf.

The mother who had been sewing fishing nets, looked up to see her son go under. She stood, paused and then ran into the surf, pushed her body harder and harder into the drag. She didn't stop until she stood on the sandbar.

The mother submerged as far as the water would let her. She pushed against the water, at the point her lungs would give out if she went further.

It was like a glass partition that prevented her from going beyond her body's limit.

Her son was there, at the bottom of the sea. He was walking still and picking up clams to inspect them. Then, the full crush of the water fell into his lungs. She watched him thrash and try to swim. The boy struggled and then floated suspended out of reach. The mother watched the current take him slowly south.

She pounded and pounded downward, punched at the making of our people—the salt in our blood that made us who we are. The water in her eyes crashed through the lens and blurred the image of her son. She surfaced for a gasp and then plunged in again.

Everyone gathered on the shore. Then the other mothers fought their way into the water and out to her. They too submerged as far as the water would let them, saw the boy's progress south, trapped near the sea bed.

They held each other and shrieked. They pulled at the woman and tried to restrain her. She lunged away from them, further and further out into the water. As she ran the sandbar along the first cliff's drop off, the others stopped following. They knew they could not stop her.

The boy's body was kept whole by the mother's emotion. He did not fall apart. Crabs did not come to him, or sharks.

She was the only woman known to have gone past the warm teal water, past the cooler blue, out to swim the deepest black. The only one, before me.

9.

The father of the boy who drowned did not go into the water again. He did not go to his wife as she dove out past the swells and disturbances of current. He did not follow her as she tracked their son's movement south, towards the Equator; as she slept curled into kelp beds, or removed her clothing to allow her body its full sleekness in the water, in its pursuit of the son.

When he learned from the others it was his son who had been taken under, and that his wife, now of single mind, was in the sea, he walked away from the village. He took nothing with him.

The windows and doors of their home remained open. The others felt a superstitious danger in closing them, that closing them would somehow keep the man and woman forever from the house and from each other. The house stayed open and parrots began to use the kitchen chairs as roosts. There were great lizards in the bathroom.

The man and woman didn't return, not in a week, not in a month. Without talking about it, the neighbors closed the front door. They left the windows in the front room open.

People said the man lost his inability to drown and became a normal man, and that is why he never returned. They said this happened the moment he heard his wife's panic. He did not want to see if it was true. They said he blamed himself for the boy's drowning, that something inside of the father had changed.

It occurred to the father to doubt his ability to be suspended inside water. This doubt became realized in his son.

10.

The story flashes into me as I stand with Samira at the edge of morning.

I brace for the plunge downward and how much terror I will feel for Samira as I bring her down with me, her huge mouth open and sucking in water, drowning more quickly than I, who knew to keep my mouth shut until the lights grew behind my lungs and forced all breath from me. The hammer of the water could come then, after I had seen her eyes rolling.

I lift my feet from where they stand on the sandbar and use my arms in wide circles to keep my head above water. I pedal my feet like they taught me as a child. Samira keeps walking the same pace as I flail behind her. She pulls me along.

Put your feet down, I say to myself. *Put your feet down.*

I can't risk swimming if my doubt finds force and my

toes sink into the water instead of stubbing on that boundary.

I feel the pull and swell of a strong current, and then Samira's line is taut under my arms—she is at the full extension of its length. There is water in her mouth. Using the line, I pull myself to her and lift her great head out of the water. The sea drains from her. I shake her head, place my face against her nose. There is breath, but it is shallow.

I heave my shoulder under her neck, hope to turn her body upright. She does not turn. I cannot tell if the current is pulling us further out or if we have by chance caught one that brings us closer to land. It wants to pull us under, but my body won't let it. There are masses of seaweed and driftwood and plastic bottles carried around us in the motion. The drum on its thin cord around my neck cuts into the skin and chafes me.

The drum's wood is sealed with sap and coal tar. The skin was chosen in ceremony. Many whole skins of cows are brought before my dad, and he selects a hide that will be stretched and weathered until it can be tuned. He was the only drummer before I received a hand-me-down and began my training. My father, the holy one, the one the sea spoke through in the voice of the drum.

The skate's egg purses are still inside. I dump them out and then force the drum under Samira's head. She takes a gasp of air and foam comes out of her nose.

I must turn our bodies against the current; I must get us off this riptide.

11.

Last winter, I snuck into the grove the night of the yearly blessing of the salt in our bodies.

It was a more casual ceremony than I expected. I thought there would be songs with words I didn't understand. But it was more like a bonfire with family. They sang a few songs and my dad played the drum. There were two rattles. My dad had his eyes closed. I closed mine too because he told me you feel the pulse more deeply that way.

I saw colors and flashes of the sea in a storm, and then how the sea looked from my front windows. I could see the fish in the shallows and as the music brought me further from the shore, I saw the tuna and mackerel I ate every day. The colors of the water continued to get brighter the further I walked out. I hoped to see whales or dolphins. There was nothing though, just light and buoyancy. And then there was just light. As my mind hung on at the edges, I realized I had dropped into the water. I was fully inside it. I had no fear.

Is this how we stay suspended? I thought. *These songs and rhythms performed yearly to keep our blood strong enough to carry our weight?*

A centipede crawled over my leg and those hundred legs stirred me. I watched it continue on the amber, pine-needled ground—grotesque and shining in the bonfire's light.

My dad was still there, as was one of the women who shook a rattle. Their low laughter did not hold secrets. I watched them: my dad was a man instead of a father. The rattler was the baker. They talked and nothing was wrong. It changed the way I saw him though. He was capable of being a person, of anything.

Did I want to see my father with that woman? Did I want to catch him doing something wrong? In that moment when I woke from the movement of many legs, I had no idea I would be different, that all conversations would hold possibility.

I realized it was me, not my dad, who had been made new.

I wanted to know more about the blood in me that did not carry salt. I wanted to know about the muscles and bones. I wanted to find a place where everyone sinks. This moment of waking led to my movement away from family, from tradition.

12.

Samira remains unconscious when I climb on top of her. Seated on her above the water, I look in all directions for land. Unless it is the curve of light at this time of late afternoon, there is a black line on the horizon in the opposite direction we are being pulled.

I slide off her side and into the water between her legs. I put my head against her stomach and my hands on either side of my head. My right hand brushes her swollen nipples. My stomach heaves at their redness.

I use all the force I can to push her sideways, head first into the current, and then keep pushing by pedaling my feet, powering off the sea's resistance.

The current seems to give. I keep pushing and turn her body in the direction of land. I will be the one to walk her back home.

13.

She comes to consciousness and then retreats. I see the slightest black of her eye between her lashes and then the lids shut. At least I know she is breathing. The drum that carries her head sometimes catches and rebounds her breath. I hear it like two exhales over the now calm water. Her inhales so shallow they don't percuss.

I scan for any shore that is not home. I will drag the floating cow there. Her chafed nipples rise and fall in the water, moving like a pink anemone.

Think of the tongue that cleaned her son; cleared his eyes of crust, smoothed down the hair on the space between his ears; taught him to lean into her when he drank and then curled herself around him after he was full and tired. She slept with her head resting on his hips.

I hadn't noticed the temperature changing in the water until the tide cut through, bringing water from other seas. The riptide brought us back to the familiar. It brought us to our ledges and deeps, to our sandbar and shore.

Tiny cleaning fish have attached themselves to my callouses. My feet are numb to the bites. I wiggle one from my heel and try to make it attach to Samira's udder. It swims away instead. I try again with the rest of them. After all swim away, one circles back and takes onto her. It can send some signal to the others that they should come clean.

She is swimming. She is swimming toward that black line.

14.

The rainbow clams try to burrow into my hand. I feel their feet pressing into the fleshy part of my thumb. They continue to try even though my hand gives them resistance. In their minds, they continue to push because everything must give. They do not know what to do without pushing.

They stop and hang suspended in the wet sand. I wonder if I've killed them. Worn their little hearts out. Burst their lungs. I spread the sand thin so I can see their shapes and the pastels: purple, pink, blue, white, cream, yellow, orange. They are all there, about double the size of a grain of rice.

I put my hand into the water, just under the surface. The motion sways them out of my hand as the silt filters, becoming less and less sand and more and more water until my hand is empty. I brush it with the other to get the last bit of sand out of the folds.

The clams will sink to the floor and again bury, this time to a place that will support them. If I killed them by not being sand, by being a hand that did not give, they will float and move through the shallows until they sink and rest on the bottom instead of in it.

I dive my hands into the sand to find crabs. I feel a large one push away from my hand. It gets away. I scoop two large handfuls of sand and again feel animals pushing down, trying to find darkness and to be in a place that is right for their bodies.

The water is like that for me, but not entirely. When I am in it, I am not of it. The water repels me. You can look at it both ways. It supports me too.

I have a dream of sky-beaten, salt-bloated Samira dead on the beach. I have nothing to give her.

15.

I can't walk back to my house with this ruined cow and
go back to my room, back to sitting with my mom and
gutting the fish my father brings.

In that world the fish arrive lifeless, already gasped
out, eyes clouded with affixation or brain bashing,
skull or neck snapping. Bodies of guts, covered in silver that scales under fingernails. Skin creates a graft
of bone or calcium to cover it, to seal out the water
that keeps them living. Bodies wrapped that need to be
unwrapped with a knife.

The bucket at our feet is full by 11AM and set down
by the water where the men enter and return from
swimming.

The smoked fish are not descaled. I carry them, finger
hooked inside their now hollow bodies, into the cedar-
lined house so dense in its smoke and outrageous in
its heat.

We wash our hands as a group, together always, a small blessing of thanks performed. When the soapy water is thrown out behind the shed, it gleams with bubbles and scales.

Cats come, drawn by the oils.

They find the bitter and foamy place.

16.

The patterns of the scales identify what they are made of. Bone, teeth, skin, cartilage—all of it living and growing.

Scales are like teeth in the water. They cut the body from the water, ramp into the body's bloodstream and skin structure.

Imagine being scaled. The light does not reach your skin. It must fight through the bone fiber, nose cartilage fiber, down into the blood. The scaled do not need the same vitamins. All that saltwater enamel shines under the surface. The quiet compactness of growing plates of teeth with muscle attached.

The bone–scaled fish are louder under the water. The bones shift and creak as the fish move their fins and tails.

I can put my ears under the water and tell which fish are near.

17.

My heart beat unnoticed until it syncopated.

I played it on the drum for my father, who took me to the doctors, who listened and did not hear it. I played it for them too. They did not want the drum in the clean room, not with its pine needles and sap pulse, leather bindings and palm oils. I played my resting heart beat for them and then played the pulsing syncopation.

"It feels like that, too," I told them.

"Like my heart has lost interest, or has been distracted and then it loses its place in the song. I can feel it jumping back into rhythm."

The man did not write this down.

I was stuck with cords and cold adhesive while the machine measured my electricity. Again nothing. All of my body was running with the same current. There were no congested stops.

I felt the syncopation again while watching the egrets nest in the tallest, oldest cedars. Their mating plumage overhung the edge of the messy, thatched nests. I wanted to catch the feathers after they dropped from the birds after their season. I never found one. The sun held the feathers in illumination as it passed through the canopy.

And again in the collection of clams on the sandbar as I raked the bed, standing barefoot in muddy silt and caught the light off the ridged and cream-colored rows of bodies.

And terns rushing and then retreating from the surface of the sea. The pulsing became a way I felt the world and the way my body connected to what it saw. I never told my dad how often it happened. It didn't hurt and the doctors didn't find it. They wouldn't find it when they looked again.

They would have to be with me when I water-walked the sandbar and saw the beauty of millions of fish moving together in a river within the waves. Or wearing goggles and hanging suspended in shallows, watching the patterns of sand placed and displaced in ridges under the surf, and how those ridges mirrored the action at the surface, where our bodies felt it.

18.

I see Samira chewing her new cud, the first food other than seaweed. There are deep red rose hips she can eat. I pull them from the plant without too much trouble. I bring some of the remaining flowers too. I imagine they are sweet.

Samira takes the offerings between her prehensile lips and crunches down. They are barely chewed before she swallows them. I see the crimson get crushed and then tongued back into her throat.

They should give her a little moisture, but I could pick five pounds of them and she would still be hungry.

The grasses slice my palms and fingers as I pull them out of the loose soil. The rose leaves also scratch my fingers with their rough edges.

I will find the mountain and sit at the base. I will see what shakes.

I will swim and be at the summit, suspended over it in a drove of constant krill and sea current, hoping for a single radiant shrimp or the glint of a scale from the deep, like a star from a sister galaxy.

I will return to the water.

19.

Before I took her, the sea was only a constant whoosh in the shell of her ear. The waves were the way the world sounded, until they became the world.

Days ago, there, where the wave is thinnest on the shore, and sand and water are equal parts wave, Samira first heard the distinction. She then understood the sound her ears had heard every day from her birth; heard and never had to understand. Before stepping into the ocean with me, the world was bells; grains falling; shearing grass; a calf sucking; hay bales; whirring insects; egrets picking mites behind her ear. The water, the whoosh, behind it all.

I took her into the water with me, selfishly. To provide for me. To be my companion so I didn't leave alone.

Samira's dark eyes are calm, but not quiet.

The air has not cut off the sap in the trees or in the roots. *Samira, you will not be hungry soon.*

I walk ahead of her. She does not resist. Her head is not down, but it is not lifted either. Her neat, hoofed feet make their crescent moons in the fine red dust of the membrane between the cedars and the beach. The land breezes bring biting flies and mosquitos to Samira's thick thighs and shivering neck muscles.

20.

Days ago, days. My feet on the bottom of the tub felt the voices of my family on the first floor. The soles felt the sounds as words, but since the foot is not an ear, the foot could not translate.

They felt the pulsing punctuation of my mother's singing to the pair of sparrows she kept in an iron cage near the front window. That window got the best, most direct light and the birds bring the light into the cage of the house. My feet could not pick up their low trill and low hum of their beaks as they cleaned and bit the other.

Every now and again my brother's affirmation or some other solid single syllable came through. My father was not home so I did not hear my father. His sounds are like my mother's: counted and paced like a recital for when the fish begin to change patterns and cannot avoid the nets. The sounds are caught in the spaces designed to catch them. Fish as words, as sounds.

I released my head from between my knees and returned to the full rush. The first sound I heard was the sea. The second was my body shifting in freshwater. I cannot go anywhere without water following.

21.

I will walk at night through the forest I know well. I can take off her bell, or stuff it with mud to deaden the tongue. She'd be back in her pen, with her son, in the morning.

And me? Stay and fish the private empire of the shallows? Eat from the nets my mother sewed, and my brother threw? The cold fingers and packed ice; the still-warm guts; the slice of bony scales under fingernails?

What life will be there for me?

I take Samira's weathered and sea-beaten rope into my calloused hand. The rope fits into the palm with a familiar weight. The skin of the pads grabs onto its fibers. A deep breath escapes from me. The heat of the breath blows onto Samira's cone-shaped ear. She twitches it and then turns it slightly back, toward me. She's waiting to hear what I do next.

I am waiting for each minute to bring us a little less light. I don't know what she is seeing in her minutes. She is most likely better at picking up on the changing light, seeing it grade into finer and finer shades of darkness.

In the coming darkness, I wait to walk her back to the barn where she was born.

What about one night here? I ask her. I've brought her deep into the woods and to the warm clay of the monastery's walls. Again her ears flick in quick movements of startle and alarm. I leave her tied around a tree along the back wall of the monastery and then circle around to the great cedar door.

It's locked.

My lower back feels like there are seeping places. I'm grateful to find a monk's cloak tossed near the entrance. I slide it over my body and keep the hood up to cover my head.

It was my father's drum that brought me out on this trip. I had been lulled to sleep by it and then woken to find his drum silent, the world fuller with possibility. If

I hadn't felt the world open to the space between my father and the baker, maybe I would have never imagined something else for myself, something outside of my role as daughter.

If.

Samira is still lying down when I turn the corner. I walk up to her slowly and then gently curl into her middle. She allows this. Maybe I will keep her a little warmer too.

She shakes her head and her bell sounds, then is silent.

Monk

1.

The star-shaped one, the triangle, the precise spokes of another. The basic circle.

The quatrefoil.

And my favorite, the corona Anthony seldom removes, the crescent tight around the bald dome of his skull; the corona that is almost blue instead of golden. Blue in the way of glaciers—both blue and not. Both colorless and sky-full.

It is smallest, but it illuminates the hollows under his dark eyes, catches the white hairs in his eyebrows, glides down the slope of his nose, and shadows the philtrum before curving light over his bottom lip.

His light brings my eyes up from the tilled rows of the garden or from the neat lines of our prayers. Brings my eyes up to meet his, which are also raised instead of humbled.

His eyes assess me coolly before he returns to peeling beets. His hands bleeding purple-red around skinned globes.

2.

Anthony wounds the largest cedar, the one just outside the clay walls of his monastery. His peeling knife flicks at the knobby bark, not deep, but enough to bring resins—the tree's way of healing itself—to the surface.

He keeps watch over our pharmacy, dispenses small balls of the sticky red resin when someone is sickened. When placed in warm water, it dissolves into a fragrant tea that speaks to the offending pith inside a body. Speaks to it and sends it on.

His personal garden is small and filled with skullcap and lemon balm. Tonics for nerves. I wonder if the light his body emits is fed by these herbs or if they feed only the parts the light does not know. Like the back of his earlobe dusted with loam after a distracted hand brushed away a fly.

What does the light know of how I want to reach and make that skin clean?

I hear the men walking in step behind me. The eldest swats me on the nape of my neck with his robe's tassel. It stings, and I am back.

3.

Silence means the click of thumbnail against wooden rosary, the turning of thin pages, the crack of old knees genuflecting. The scrape of metal spoon against ceramic bowl.

The shuffle, the limp, the hustle of ambulation. Coughs, sneezes, sniffles.

Silence means the wet hesitation of resistance a potato makes with each pass of the knife. The dry rip of collard greens removed from their stalk.

It is hearing a throat swallowing milk. A throat swallowing tea. The dry sockets of teeth chewing bread.

It is hearing the air around hands as they perform ritual, as all men move in the same pattern. A touch to the forehead, to the heart, to the shoulders. As hands come together to touch palms.

Silence means hearing the fabric around our bodies, the swish of robes. It is the strike of a match and the fizz of flame catching. Of breath ending flame before it reaches fingers.

The moon-fed movements of the ocean and its response through the cedars. The falling of those cedar's needles or the thump of the cones.

And always the *tsk tsk* of straw brooms cleaning some corner, some hallway.

Silence means hearing bodies turning in narrow beds, the scrabble of mice feet and the muted whoosh of a raptor.

*

This silence meant I was not alone.

4.

There is one road out and it leads to the ocean. Each winter I spend one day walking this road, one day collecting seaweed for our gardens.

I pack bread and roasted beets to smash into a white loaf and drizzle with honey. Even when there were many of us, this was always my job. I was not happy to see the world I had newly left. But the resentment did not last.

The ocean is gray and white-capped. The beach roped with black branches of bladder wrack. There are hundreds of whelk shells of all sizes. Their spirals are intact despite the force it took to throw them up on the shore.

I imagine their deaths: hordes of starfish moving their tubular bodies over the bottom of the ocean towards the animals whose shells are meant to protect their slowness. The shells fail against the teeth and stomachs of the starfish. All of these dead on the beach, the soft parts of their bodies gone to feed other bodies.

Seaweed to feed the soil of the gardens that sustain us. Red, brown, green-black. Stiff and brittle. Feathery and webbed. The dried pieces are too light and the wind lifts them from the cart. I'm driven to the waterline, to retrieve heavier branches.

The wet plants make my arms and hands sticky. Grains of sand roll up under my fingernails. As water dries on my robe, it leaves salt and sand in pale tracks.

A line of brown pelicans moves low over the water. Because of my stillness, ghost crabs begin to emerge from their holes.

They push out the sand that fell in as they rushed to safety.

One of them, midsize, takes great pains to make a neat mound. It brings out the sand cradled in the large claw, and then tamps it down instead of throwing it. Something in the small animal's pride of working, if I can call it that, reminds me of my mother.

The wooden boards with the nails pounded into fine patterns. I knew not to touch them, not to disrupt the quiet motion they contained.

She would move that thread around the tiny nails, looping and winding and tying small knots, over and over until the thread built up upon itself and became something you could hold.

Her bones memorized the movements. She could look up at me as I walked in the door and continue her work.

The lace brought money that added to the money she made as a housekeeper. My mother with the hands of a ghost crab.

5.

I hide a small whelk in the pocket of my robe. I am not to have possessions, and this counts as one.

Where will I hide it when I'm back? Inside the frame of the bed, under the mattress. What a lot of trouble to have a small, dead piece of animal. But still, I want it.

It stays tucked into the deepest fold of the pocket, where sand and lint collects.

6.

My first winter Anthony could not find a fever in me. There was no headache, no body aches. But I could not leave my bed.

He took my jaw in his right hand and stuck out his tongue, miming what he needed me to do. I compiled, watching his eyes scan my tongue for ridges, papules, and coatings to see where my blood was moving and where it was stuck.

Satisfied, he released my jaw and stepped away.

I had been eating soda crackers and thin broth. Using a bedpan like an elderly monk. I had been watching my sleepless self appear in outline on the wall as the sun rose. If I had wanted to, I could have talked to this shadow.

Anthony appeared with a small packet of dried mushrooms, licorice root and tiny rose buds. On a slip of paper he had written the correct ratio of material to hot water and the frequency of consumption.

His eyes did not ask after me. *Cry into your pillow* is what his shoulders said.

The sickness lifted, but my brain felt slow and damaged, blunted and shallow, for weeks.

7.

Never mind the ghost crabs cleaning their holes and making lace patterns with their feet. The ghost crabs and the seaweed cannot make lace like my mother.

She sees the pattern of light through the thinnest of supports. The light pushes through the thread and shows what is missing. It is the holes that make lace. The thread is there to hold up the missing, to point it out. This is the way our lungs look when you shine a light through the chest. The heart does not effuse like this.

Not like the wooden board with pin nails to guide the thread into the patterns, a magnifying glass attached to the bridge of her glasses. Her pointer finger dry and chapped from the pulling, rolling of thread through loops.

8.

I watched him weed dandelions from a row of cabbage. His trowel went in deep, at the angle he taught me, so the trowel would lift and cut the root. He wrapped a handkerchief around the seeded head so the fluff wouldn't spread, carefully, as if capturing a trapped bird. He placed the root in a bucket reserved for his medicines and folded the seed head into his pocket.

There was a spasm in the movement of his wrist. A moment when something else passed through and was gone.

He turned to me, his six coronas glowing. I felt their light on my downturned face. I did not look up.

Later, I passed by his door to see if the silence contained him. I had dreams of speaking the first weeks.

9.

I haul my cart to the empty and plowed under garden beds. Taking the seaweed in my hands, I then throw it over the rows, and dive my shovel into the loamy mess to force the new into the old.

The soil is rich and dark. The sea is there, so slightly, in the taste of the greens we grow.

My hands red and chapped like my mother's. The whelk shell bumps into my thigh as I dig. The sensation jolts me each time. The secret thrums my heart. I picked something from the world and kept it.

My eyes catch the current of sea birds over the monastery. They catch on the storm surge and wind lashings, the cedars with their sap-colored skin. The birds overhead are not embarrassed by hunger.

The important thing is to hide the whelk and hide it in my face too. It can't be hidden in my room and open in my face.

Is this small dead thing worth this sweat?
Would a piece of my mother's lace be worth it?

I knew that if I failed here, I would not return to town. My mother would never know, because I'd be somewhere else, working the docks like I did as a boy. On some other coast. My mother could be proud of the faith of her son.

All my life, all I have done is work and listen to the radio. My only contribution is you, she had said.

I might as well been a womb without a body.

You did not just work, I said.

She shrugged and clipped the magnifying glass back onto the rim of her glasses.

10.

I did not hear what the eldest monk said, but I saw his mouth lower to Anthony's right ear, and I saw the mouth move. Anthony's eyes rose to meet the monk's. They stayed there until the monk turned and left down the darkened hallway.

Yellow calendula staining my fingers.

He pushed himself back from the table, upsetting the tinctures. His robes around his body in a noisy vortex.

His light made a candle unnecessary.

*

The bell tower housed seagulls who circled and cried when I disturbed them. The coronas turned to look, to watch the white bodies in the sky, to see what could have woken them.

He again started into the cedars, down the path that he had worn to the stream that fed into the ocean. And then the coronas were moving separately from his body—the triangle skipping across the surface of the stream. It bounced twice before spinning and sinking into the current. He tried again with the circle and got four skips before the light sunk and traveled downstream.

The two points of light moved with the dark water and were out of sight. I stood on the railing to look toward the ocean, to see if I could catch them merging into that body. My hand slipped, and I struck the bell with my full weight.

The old clapper rang against the metal and I felt it through my teeth, conducting through my blood into the hollows of my chest.

I felt sound opening silence, peeling it back again and again as it announced my frailty.

11.

I rose early and went to put on tea. I walked by his room and saw the door was open. The bed made.

I entered and looked for a note. Just a bed, a table and a chair. Empty drawers, closet. I sat on the bed and felt a rush of expectation leave.

Goodbye, I said aloud to the room.

It was the first word I had spoken in years. I turned to look around me—my voice and the impulse to speak were so far removed, I had to confirm it was me.

I cleared my throat.
Goodbye, I said again.

I heard a slight shifting of plates in the kitchen. I rose. The kitchen was empty.

I went back to bed, but didn't sleep until the sun began to rise. In those predawn hours, I shifted in bed, hearing only the goat's bell moving a slow rhythmic chime as she chewed whatever sweet grass Anthony had left her.

A kindness to the goat, a present. When the sun came up, sheared through the room, I turned from it and slept.

12.

The chafe of salt, wind, and wooden handle on my already chapped hands brings cracks in the knuckles and small splits of blood around my cuticles.

I take my clogs off near the kitchen door, and feel the cold of the slate on my damp feet. The kettle cannot warm quickly enough.

Hot water is rushed onto tea leaves and sipped before it is flavorful. I am grateful for warmth and steam.

In a mixing bowl, I pour the rest of the hot water, and drop a bar of soap in to get a good film going. The water stings and prickles the tips of my fingers as circulation returns. It stings the cracks in my knuckles.

In my pocket, the small whelk hums.

The sudden heat in my throat and on my hands makes me sleepy. The sweat has dried on my neck and temples.

Those places still feel cold.

The water smells of the sea. My hands absorb it in their calluses. A briny residue on my wrists. I think of the fine patterns of light on the main road.

My hips pull at my lower back, and I think of the warm baths at my mother's, where the water was not piney-red and mineral cold.

It comes to me that my sickness that first winter could have been from something as small as the memory of my boyhood body in a warm bathtub.

I continue to soak my hands. I have no idea if my mother is still alive and sitting on that plaid couch with the radio.

The water drying on my arms and chest starts the chill. The rag has collected the sweat and skin and is at last rubbed onto my shoulders and upper back, because it is there the chill sets in deepest.

I had to unlearn many things about the way the body was treated at home.

This is not to say the pleasure of the mind wasn't enough. Most days it was. Most days the light behind my eyelids as I prayed was enough to push aside the body. Most days it was enough to lean into that yawn of light.

But now I crawl into bed and tuck the covers behind my neck. Even after the washing, my body smells of the sea. There are places the soap did not gather the salt. It is possible, I realize, that the sea is in my nose, in sand and salt warmed into fragrance. I will blow it out later. For now I allow my body to want what it wants.

13.

One of the monks went without anything that would soften the bread and make it easier to chew. Or anything that would release pleasure, like butter. I knew to press the buttered bread to the roof of my mouth, so the tongue covered the most area, to let it absorb the fat and then begin to chew. That same monk would not bathe, but no one motioned to him to soap up. We ate with our noses closed and ate tasteless meals.

The monk had a wild eye that roamed the table and then roamed the ceiling. Sometimes both of them were wild and you could see a voice in his head coming out of his eyes and into our ears.

He stunk of scalp oil even though he had almost no hair.

These talking eyes were full of voices. I could see the voice of God and of men.

When this monk cooked, he liked to use seaweed to bring in umami. It seemed to be his only bodily concession. I learned to save some for him. He dried it, and crushed it into a powder with a mortar. It was contained in a small glass container with a cork lid.

After he left, I moved the container under the sink.

The idea grew. Unlike Anthony, the monks talked before they left. The air was different after their voices. Speech hung where none had for decades. I could hear their voices when I looked at them, even when they were silent.

I lick the corners of my mouth into two red crescent moons. My tongue wants to speak, reaches the rim of the mouth and has to stop. It goes to the corners in a retreating way, like a dog who has lunged and been pulled back by a chain.

14.

The cedars' sap has started to run, spring driving the minerals up to the first push of new green needles, and sending sugar made from those thin leaves down. The sapwood flush with new activity.

I stand at the largest dune.

A flock of oystercatchers rest on the beach. Their black heads are set off by their white underbellies and the red-orange of their long beaks. They have yellow eyes rimmed in red. They are clustered together; their chests on the sand to get out of the wind.

I've never seen so many together.

The tiny bell around the goat's necks chimes in the wind. The birds see us but do not move.

We walk into a fine spray. It is impossible to tell which direction it is coming from. The beach or the sky. Or from both at once and also the ground and the air itself, all mixing and settling into my clothes and the goat's fine whiskers.

Sit, I say to the goat.
She does not sit.

I sit and try to pull her down with me. She bucks away, prongs to the end of her rope and strains her neck until she is as close to the ground as she can get with her feet still planted. I do not let up on the rope.

The sand is damp beneath me and comes right through the fabric of my pants.

All of those days and years within the monastery, all of the sameness contracts and then expands away. The world is back to being how it truly smells—not only the closeness of bodies and small meals or hay and fermenting manure. The world comes full into our noses.

The goat and I are the same in this expanding. I walk to her and untie the rope.

I can now choose my own schedule. I don't have to think of it as a schedule. I can think of it as time, as a day. The day opens up before me like the summer does for a child.

The wet collects on my face and in my eyebrows. My hands go up to the baldness of my head. I will miss the hands of monks who held my head straight, or to the side, tilting it to get the scissors as close to the scalp as possible.

The goat walks up the beach to the tough grasses.

I look out to the open breakers. There is a girl beyond them; she has seen me before I saw her. As our eyes meet, she turns and heads further out to sea.

She does not wait long to look back. Once she sees I've gotten up and come closer to the water's edge, she retreats more. There appears to be something huge and white and muscular beside her.

I start to doubt myself.
The world is stranger than I remember.

Every now and again I see her head, or what I think is her head. Sometimes it is a pelican's buoyant body. I lose focus on the water coming at me, and a wave rushes past the others to soak me up to my ankles. As it recedes, I feel the sandy foam sink into my low clogs, into my socks. The slow creep will make its way to my toes.

I didn't bring anything with me. Not a single change of clothes or extra socks. It felt better leaving like that.

No robe either. I left that by the outer door.

There is a man on the beach a ways down. The wind carries the smell of sardine oil fresh in the pan of his fire. Gulls start their slow, unstable walk toward him. I can see the red rim of their yellow eye even from here. The sardine smell must be heaven.

The man at the camp does not look at them. He can sense their movement and every so often, throws an arm back in a violent shooing. His eyes are on the water, on the head in the water way out near the shelf.

15.

Yes, in the monastery we were aware of our mouths and the muscles of our faces. The smallest turn of a corner down or up called into question the taste of the soup or praised the laundry for its sweet cleanness. And the bodies turned off to gratification and sensation became alive with it. Without the touch of others, our bodies learned to feel the cloth instead of just wear it.

Faces told us feelings, but shoulders did too.

I read the man's shoulders silhouetted by fire. He has plenty of wood to keep it going and to keep the coals hot enough to restart it easily in the morning.

Just a pan to cook the fish and the kettle for coffee, two mugs, two plates. A flannel blanket over his knees and lower legs. A blue tarp rolled up behind him.

"My daughter," he says and gestures out to the waves, "I've been keeping an eye on her for a few days."

The rest of the beach is dark. The moon is not full and what crescent there is, is half hidden. The water is black, with rolling grays for white caps and deep purples for the spill up on the beach.

Gold comes through every so often and hits the far ocean, the deep outer space of it.

There is no girl.

16.

My feet take me up through the dunes to the compacted trail. The cedars around me like druids. The door I thought I knew is locked.

I circle the monastery the way I first did when I arrived. Now when I look at the clay walls, my mind sees the comb of halls and our prismatic cells. I continue the circumambulation around the farthest corner. There is a huge white cow next to the largest cedar's trunk.

She is sleeping with her head between her legs, like a dog. Her body is beautiful.

There is a ball of brown curled into the cow's side, with the hood of robe up over the head.

What monk brought me a cow?
What monk will see me unrobed?

The shame is searing. My first impulse is to turn away,

to hide my face. But the promise of brotherhood again starts my feet toward him.

I nudge his shoulder with my foot. The thin body moves easily under the slight pressure. His head rolls into the cow's stomach, which exposes the infected, scabby udders.

The man jumps awake.

The hood falls back. A girl's eyes meet mine and focus in surprise. She collects her body up onto the cow, sits on the rib cage. The cow shifts under her, rotates its head back to watch the girl. The shifting pushes the girl off, but she catches her balance and stands, the cow between us. And then the cow heaves its body upward, a moon among the cedars.

The girl does not speak. She settles her weight against the cow and tries to comfort it. The cow does not respond well to her touch.

It moans, stretches its neck up as long as it will go and expands its throat, opening the mouth to extend the tongue. Air is walloped inside her mouth as it is forced in and then out.

And then it is running. Running through cedars, dragging the heavy rope as it collects needles and brush. Nothing slows it.

There is something of the sea in the girl's face, changing and dark.

I reach for her wrist, and then her forehead. Both are cool and damp. Her hair is wet and stuck to her cheeks. I push it away. Her face softens some at my touch. Her jaw relaxes.

It is only out of concern that I touch. Not affection. I test my voice.

Hello, I say. I sound unfamiliar.

My ears did not remember well what I sound like. The voice is deeper and fuller, like it continued to age without me knowing.

Hello, I say again.

It sounds like I am using someone else's voice. There is an accent of silence.

She watches my mouth move and is not surprised. She looks out toward the beach. The cow has stopped crying and I can no longer hear its body crashing through the forest.

I watch the girl's face. There is no voice in her. No words in her mind. There is no voice in her mind.

Moonlight plays off the smooth scar on her cheek. Like a fishing hook caught her long ago. The salt on her body is so thick it flakes off. Her lips are cracked.

I take her hand. She allows this. She follows me down the path toward the ocean. When we break from the cedars, light opens over the water.

The man's fire smells sweet from the pine's fresh sap cracking. I see his smoke from the distance of the road.

She lets go of my hand and walks the rest of the way to the man's camp. I watch until I see him leap up and embrace her. She sinks into my man's body.

I turn back to the forest to find an overturned tree, to sleep in the pit its death made.